THE MYSTERIOUS CAMPER

by Ruth Johnson Jay

A
BACK TO THE BIBLE
PUBLICATION

Back to the Bible
Lincoln, Nebraska 68501

10,000 printed to date—1980
(5-9578—10M—110)
ISBN 0-8474-6305-2

Printed in the United States of America

Contents

Content

Chapter 1

Off to Arizona

Karen Tyler peered into the already crowded station wagon and pushed the last piece of luggage into the only available spot. The trip to Arizona was going to be fun, she was sure of that, but it was also going to be long and uncomfortable with all the camping equipment and flannelgraph material taking up so much of the space. And with Roy Sparton's and her brother Dave's luggage plus her dad's traveling bag, there was hardly any room for her three suitcases. Dave teased her unmercifully, insisting that she was taking altogether too much stuff, but there was absolutely nothing she could do without! Absolutely nothing! She was sure of it.

With hundreds of miles to travel, the ride would be much more comfortable if they could take their own car, but then her mother would have no means of transportation while they were gone. And then, too, the trunk of the family car was not nearly big enough to hold everything they were taking. So the church-owned station wagon would have to do.

Karen hadn't really wanted to go along for the church's Vacation Bible School assignment in Arizona. She had visualized a summer of swimming and fun. But when Mrs. Black had called and told them how they had accepted more chil-

5

dren than they had planned to and needed another person to work with the girls, Karen had consented to go. And since her father's business was taking him to nearby Mexico, he had agreed to drive the three teenagers down to the rustic Arizona Bible camp.

"Man, this is sure going to be one great week," Dave Tyler said enthusiastically after they were well on their way. "The first thing I want to do is look up one of those copper mines. I guess they're really something."

Roy Sparton shook his head vigorously.

"That's not for me," he answered. "I've read all about the snake dances and tribal ceremonies and things some of the Indian tribes have down there. That's what I want to see."

Karen wrinkled up her nose in disdain.

"Snake dances? Copper mines?" she repeated. "Why would anyone want to waste time seeing those things? Don't you know the people are famous for their basket weaving and blankets and jewelry and things? I promised Mom I'd bring her something the people there have made."

Mr. Tyler had been silent while the young people were discussing their plans for the week. However, as soon as there was a lull in the conversation, he spoke up.

"You kids aren't forgetting why you're going down there, are you?" he asked. The smile on the corners of his mouth assured the teens that he was not scolding, only reminding them of their first responsibility.

"No, Dad," Dave replied. "We're not forgetting. But when Mr. and Mrs. Black first wrote, they told us there'd be time for hikes and sight-seeing after the sessions."

"And it'll be part of our camp activity too," Roy reminded him.

"I know," Mr. Tyler laughed. "I just wanted to remind you that this week isn't going to be all vacation. Bible school is going to mean a lot of good, hard work, especially since it's held on some rustic campgrounds."

They had traveled for more than two hours when Karen turned around and looked beyond the boys in the backseat and out through the back window.

"Hey, Dad," she said seriously. "That camper has been behind us ever since we left Trendale, hasn't it?"

"Yes," he said slowly. "I think you're right."

"Is it following us?" Karen asked, concern in her voice.

"Oh, I doubt it," Mr. Tyler replied. "The fact is, that camper was on the road when I pulled out from the Trendale exit."

Dave turned and looked out the back window and then tapped his sister on her shoulder.

"Hey, Karen, you always talk about becoming a writer," he said. "Why don't you make up some story about this camper—you know, some kind of scary mystery or something?"

Karen felt her anger building but tried not to let it show. She certainly couldn't let Roy Sparton see how her brother's teasing got through to her.

"Well, I'm not writing a mystery," she countered as evenly as she could. "But I still think it's strange that this camper has been traveling right behind us all this time."

7

"Doesn't seem strange to me," Dave remarked. "We're on a main highway, you know."

Karen decided to say no more about the tagging camper for the time being. What Dave said was true—they were on one of the busiest highways in the state, and traffic was pretty heavy. At the same time, she had watched as the driver of the old camper passed one car after another when someone got between them. But not once did he make a move to pass the station wagon her dad was driving. The way the driver stayed right with them almost made it seem as though they were traveling together.

Karen turned and looked at the old camper again.

"Hey, Dad," she said, a note of concern in her voice. "You don't think there's anything to worry about, do you?"

"Worry about?" Dave answered from the backseat. "Like what?"

Karen paused momentarily.

"Well, you hear about lots of things that happen on the road. People try to sideswipe you and push you off the road and—"

Dave interrupted her.

"Karen!" he nearly shouted. "I was just kidding about writing a mystery. For cryin' out loud, some guy's just going on vacation or something."

Karen was somewhat embarrassed that Dave would talk to her this way when Roy Sparton was in the car with them. But she said nothing.

During the silence, Mr. Tyler looked down at the gas gauge in the station wagon and whistled.

"Looks like this thing takes a lot more gas than

8

our car," he said seriously. "I'd better start looking for a service station."

Dave grinned. "Hey, Dad, I don't think you should put all the blame on the station wagon." He laughed as he spoke. "I think it's all that heavy luggage Karen jammed in the back that's weighing us down. And that's got to make us guzzle a lot of extra fuel."

Everyone laughed good-naturedly, even Karen.

"Hey," Roy called out after a time. "There's a service station." He pointed to a large overhead sign on the opposite side of the highway.

Mr. Tyler quickly signaled a left turn, crossed the busy left lane of traffic and pulled into the area where the gas pumps were located. As he did, Karen instinctively turned to see if the camper would follow. Yes! The driver of the camper was turning too. He was following them directly into the same service station.

"You've got to be kidding," Karen said aloud. "He's following us again."

Roy and Dave both turned around and watched as the old camper pulled into the station. But instead of parking behind them, he drove over to one of the pumps on the other side of the building.

"Well," Dave insisted casually. "Those babies use a lot of gas."

But Karen Tyler was not convinced.

"But doesn't it seem odd that he'd pick the same station we picked, especially when Dad decided at the last minute to turn into this one?"

Roy had not involved himself in any of the family argument up to now, but he couldn't resist making a comment.

"It wouldn't be strange if he happens to carry

9

the same credit card your dad carries," he defended. "And anyway, he might have planned on stopping here long before we did."

Before Karen could disagree or the discussion could go on any longer, Mr. Tyler interrupted, suggesting that everyone get out and stretch while the station wagon was being serviced.

Karen opened the door and stepped out, all the time looking in the direction of the camper and its driver. Even from a distance she could see the license plate. The vehicle was from out of state. And as far as she could tell, the driver was traveling alone. That, too, seemed strange to the Tyler girl.

Karen ambled across to the other side of the building and stood a short distance from the camper. The driver opened a small window and instructed the station attendant to fill the large vehicle with gas.

To Karen's surprise, the camper's driver was a lady. Karen tried to look in without being too obvious, but there were curtains pulled across most of the windows. That, too, seemed strange and triggered her imagination. Maybe there were a bunch of people sleeping inside, or maybe someone was forcing the lady to drive while they kept themselves under cover.

Karen was determined to find out something about the mysterious camper before returning to their station wagon. So she stepped up to the side of the camper and looked in the small window.

"Hi," she said casually, looking up at the woman.

"Hello," the dark-haired young woman responded.

Karen stared at the young driver for several seconds before speaking again.

"You traveling?" Karen asked and then realized how stupid her question sounded. It was obvious that she was traveling. What she had really wanted to ask was if the woman was traveling alone.

"Yes," the woman replied. She said no more. In fact, it seemed to Karen that the woman acted a little nervous.

"So are we," Karen replied casually. "We're going to Arizona."

Karen wasn't sure if it was her imagination or if the woman actually showed a spark of interest at the mention of Arizona.

"That's nice," the lady answered. "I am too."

That was the first bit of information the woman had offered voluntarily. But before Karen could ask anything else, the attendant returned, asking the lady to sign her credit ticket. When she finished, she waved a hand in Karen's direction and then closed the small window. At the same moment Mr. Tyler called for his passengers to return to the station wagon so they could get on their way.

"Well, did you interrogate him?" Dave asked when Karen returned to the car.

"Interrogate?" Karen replied in mock surprise. "I was just trying to be friendly. And anyway, it's not a 'he,' it's a lady."

"You didn't get too nosey, did you?" Dave added.

Karen decided to ignore her brother's comment.

"She's going to Arizona," she said casually.

"Well, in that case, it's not too surprising that she's following us," Mr. Tyler acknowledged. "We all seem to be going the same direction."

Roy, who was sitting with Dave in the backseat, looked at Karen.

"You still think she's tagging us on purpose?" he asked after a time.

Karen nodded.

"Well, she didn't leave the station before we did," she defended. "And she still hasn't passed us." She paused momentarily. "And Dad isn't driving very fast," she continued, "so she could have passed lots of times."

Mr. Tyler laughed. "Maybe we both believe in staying within the speed limit."

For several miles Karen said little about the camper. But whenever she thought Dave was not watching her, she would look back to see if the lady was still directly behind them. The fact that the camper's windows were covered made her suspicious.

Roy saw what Karen was doing.

"I know how we can decide if she's following us," Roy broke into Karen's thoughts. "If she stops at the same campground we stop at tonight, that could be a clue."

Dave did not agree.

"Not necessarily," he retorted quickly. "She might have her trip planned just like we do. Maybe she already intends to stop overnight at the state campgrounds."

Karen had to admit that it was a definite possibility. But the more she thought about it, the more she felt the woman in the old camper was making a definite effort to stay directly behind them. The only thing the Tyler girl couldn't figure out was why.

Karen's vivid imagination began to work over-

12

time, creating various reasons for the woman to be following them. The word "hostage" was in the news all the time. It flashed wildly through Karen's mind. Maybe the lady was being forced to drive someone to Arizona. She shuddered at the thought. Surely her father would find another road to take if the camper continued to tag them throughout the day.

If only those curtains had not been closed, she could have looked in and had some idea of what was going on. Suddenly Karen shook her head. This was silly. She had to shrug off these thoughts. The lady was probably on vacation. Or maybe she was moving to another part of the country and felt more secure traveling close to a station wagon full of people. Not that the four of them made the car look that full, but all the luggage and equipment certainly did.

But try as she would, Karen could not forget the nervous, almost worried look on the woman's face. If Dave had not made so much fun of Karen for imagining such outlandish things, she would ask her father what he thought about it all.

Her father seemed to sense her concern.

"You still worried?" he asked softly, hoping the boys would not hear.

Karen nodded silently.

"As Dave said," her father continued, "this is a busy highway, and we don't really know for sure the lady is following us."

But to Karen Tyler, there was absolutely no doubt at all. They were being followed by a woman driving a mysterious old camper. That was for sure!

Chapter 2

"Two of Everything"

Everyone in the church-owned station wagon managed to curl up and go to sleep during the next hour or so of traveling; that is, everyone except Mr. Tyler. Someone had to see that they continued toward their destination.

Karen opened her eyes slowly. "Where are we, Dad?" she asked, looking out the window. The scenery looked different than it had an hour earlier.

He smiled pleasantly at her. "Oh, about 50 miles farther than we were when you started snoring."

"Snoring!" Karen retorted indignantly. "I don't snore."

Mr. Tyler laughed heartily. "Well, in that case, it had to be coming from the backseat, because someone was sawing logs, that's for sure."

At the mention of the backseat passengers, Roy and Dave began to stir.

"Hey, Dad," Dave said sleepily. "Isn't it about time to stop for lunch? Man, I'm starved."

"Yes," Mr. Tyler agreed. "I'm getting pretty hungry myself." He looked at his watch. "It's after one. You know, I passed an eating place a few miles back, but everyone in the car was sound asleep, so I didn't want to wake you up."

"But we're definitely awake now," Roy yawned. "And I go along with Dave. I'm hungry!"

14

Mr. Tyler laughed and glanced at his sleepy daughter in the front seat with him.

"How about you, Karen? You ready to eat?"

"Yeah," she said slowly. Then she remembered the camper that had been following them. She turned around quickly to look.

"She's still with us, isn't she?" Karen asked simply.

"Yes," Mr. Tyler admitted. "She's been with us the whole time. I even slowed down a few miles back just to give her a chance to pass if she wanted to."

"But she didn't?" Karen asked. There was a note of concern in her voice.

"No, she slowed down too," her dad reported. "So I think you just might have a point—about her following us."

Karen turned and looked at her brother.

"See," she said deliberately. "Dad believes me."

Dave laughed heartily.

"That's because he hasn't heard all those other mystery stories you've pawned off on us."

Karen pointed her forefinger in his direction.

"Just wait," she said emphatically, at the same time laughing. "I'll get even with you."

The conversation suddenly changed when Roy spotted the sign of an eating place.

"Open 24 hours a day," he read aloud.

"Let's stop, Dad," Dave encouraged.

With that Mr. Tyler signaled his turn and pulled into the parking lot of the highway cafe. This time it was Roy who turned to see if the mysterious tagalong was following them to the cafe.

"Well, you're still right, Karen," he said matter-of-factly. "She's turning in behind us."

15

"She sure is," Karen replied deliberately, at the same time turning to stare at her brother.

Dave laughed mechanically. "So she got hungry at the same time we did," he insisted.

"Uh-uh," Roy said, also looking at the Tyler boy. "I don't think so, Dave. I think Karen's got a point. That lady in the camper is definitely tagging us."

"Well!" Karen said sharply. "That's two on my side."

"One to go," Roy laughed, pointing his finger toward Dave Tyler. "And maybe if all of us work on him, he'll come around too."

Dave shook his head vigorously.

"No way," he insisted. "I have to have more proof than that." He paused significantly. "As far as I'm concerned, that camper is traveling on a public highway. The poor lady just needed gas the same time we did."

Karen stared at her brother in disbelief.

"And what about her stopping now?"

Dave shrugged.

"When she saw us pull into the cafe parking lot, that reminded her that she hadn't eaten. Anyway, there's no crime in following."

Karen slapped the back of her hand to her forehead.

"And you say I write mysteries. Wow!"

Mr. Tyler brought the station wagon to a stop in the parking lot, and the foursome got out and entered the nearly filled dining room. A hostess seated them in one of the few available booths and gave each of them a menu.

"Has she come in yet?" Roy asked before opening the large menu. "With my back toward the entrance I won't be able to see if she comes in."

16

Karen shook her head. "She hasn't come in yet."

In another minute a waitress came to take their orders. Then the small group sat back to relax while they waited for their dinners to be served. That is, everyone except Karen Tyler relaxed. Her eyes were focused steadily on the front door.

"Here she comes," she whispered loudly as the driver of the old camper opened the cafe door and entered the dining area.

"Is she alone?" Roy asked, a sincere interest in his voice.

Karen nodded. She still could not understand why a young woman would choose to travel on a busy highway all alone—if she was alone—and in such an old camper. Dave had the answer when she voiced her concern.

"Probably because she owns that beat-up old camper and can't afford a new one," he said offhandedly.

Suddenly a thought entered Karen's mind. She picked up her purse from the seat of the booth and started to slide out.

"I'll be right back," she said. "I'm going up to the counter to get some gum."

Roy Sparton put his hand into his shirt pocket.

"I've got some gum you can have," he said quickly.

A look of disappointment overshadowed Karen's face, but only for a second.

"Thanks, but I'd just as soon get my own brand," she said flatly. With that she left the booth and walked toward the cash register area. As she reached the counter, the lady from the camper began placing her order.

17

"Two cartons of milk and two servings of gelatin, please—to go."

Karen stepped up behind the lady.

"Hi again," she said simply.

The woman looked up and spoke and then stepped aside. Then, just as quickly, she moved forward once again and spoke to the waitress. There was an edge to her voice, and she seemed unusually nervous.

"Could I get that right away?" she asked. "I'm in a hurry."

The waitress stopped long enough to take Karen's money and give her a package of gum. Then she left to get the woman's order.

Karen took her small purchase back to the booth, a look of dismay on her face.

"That is the funniest order I've ever heard," she said, sliding back into the booth next to her father. "Two cartons of milk and two servings of gelatin."

Mr. Tyler smiled broadly.

"Sounds like she's either got an ulcer or a baby."

"Or she's broke," Roy added.

Karen continued talking, just as though she had not heard what either Roy or her father had said.

"Two of everything," she reported. "And she told the waitress she had to have her order right away because she was in a big hurry."

The waitress brought their dinners, and they all bowed their heads for prayer.

"We thank You, Lord, for a safe trip," Mr. Tyler prayed aloud. "And we also give You thanks for this food. Strengthen and nourish our bodies through it. May we use the energy we derive from it in a way that would honor You. And, Lord, as

18

You give us opportunities to witness, help us to be faithful. Amen."

Karen Tyler looked up as soon as her father had finished praying, but the mysterious woman was no longer in the cafe.

"She's gone," she said, a hint of disappointment in her voice.

Dave's patience was beginning to grow thin, and Karen sensed it.

"So why should that surprise you?" he asked irritably. "She said she was in a hurry."

Karen said no more about the mysterious woman. As the group continued to eat, the conversation changed to the opportunities that would be theirs during the next seven days at the Bible camp. Karen's enthusiasm for camp was still at a low ebb. And she wasn't sure why. She knew there would be opportunities for witnessing, but even that didn't thrill her. She thought about it for a long time.

Finally, Roy broke into her thoughts with a question.

"Is it true that Arizona has a terrific petrified forest?" he inquired.

Dave put his glass down on the table.

"That's what I've heard," he replied. "But, man, they've got a lot more things than that."

"Like what?" Roy asked, knowing all along what some of those things were.

"Like the Grand Canyon," Karen injected quickly, surprised that Roy would even have to ask such a question.

"And Hoover Dam," Dave added.

"And an active Bible camp where three young people from the Midwest will soon be working,"

19

Mr. Tyler finished. His contribution brought a round of laughter across the table, and the conversation came to an abrupt end.

Mr. Tyler reached into his pocket for a gospel tract. He left it on the table with his tip and went to pay for the dinners. The teens left the cafe and walked toward the station wagon. For the moment they had almost forgotten about the tagalong camper.

"Hey!" Roy Sparton said loudly. And then just as quickly he realized that he could be heard if he did not lower his voice. "Look, the lady—she's still there. She couldn't have been in too big a hurry."

Karen spotted the old camper still parked exactly where it had been when they went into the dining room more than 30 minutes ago. She turned and faced her brother but decided to say nothing.

Dave caught the unspoken rebuke. He shrugged his shoulders.

"OK," he said mysteriously. "So Chapter two in your mystery is coming up."

Even though Karen's mind was filled with questions, she laughed along with the others. But in spite of her laughter, she still had a strange feeling of concern that she could not dismiss. Maybe it would make sense for a woman who was traveling alone to stay close behind another vehicle going the same direction. Maybe it would make her feel more secure. But this woman was not traveling alone. If she were, why would she order two cartons of milk and two orders of gelatin?

And then, too, if she were alone, she probably would have eaten her lunch in the cafe. There would have been no reason to take it out to the

20

camper unless there was someone else in there who could not—or would not—come in.

The lady was obviously waiting for them to finish their dinner so she could follow right behind them.

Something was very strange, very mysterious about this whole situation. But Karen Tyler could come up with no answers.

Chapter 3

"We May Have Company"

The next few hours seemed to be a repeat performance of what had happened during the earlier hours of the day. Mr. Tyler always led the way, and the lady in the camper tagged along behind them. When a car would get between them, it would be only a matter of minutes before the old camper would pass and get into position again.

"Boy," Karen grumbled, thinking back to their lunch stop. "She was in such a hurry to get out of the cafe, and then she sat out there and waited for us."

Dave shook his head vigorously.

"We don't know that she waited for us," he argued. "Maybe she was sitting in there listening to her favorite soap opera or something."

"Soap operas are on TV," Karen retorted.

By this time Mr. Tyler entered the conversation.

"Are we beginning to make too much of this?" he asked warningly. He aimed his comments to all of them, but for some reason he looked squarely at Karen. "Let's not forget that we asked the Lord to guide us on our trip. And if that means having a frightened lady follow close behind us, we shouldn't get too concerned about that."

Roy Sparton nodded. "Yeah, maybe you're right, Mr. Tyler," he said. "She's probably pretty scared traveling alone. And maybe she just feels better if she's near somebody who could help her if she got into trouble."

"But she's not alone," Karen retorted. "At least I don't think she is."

Dave Tyler laughed aloud.

"Hey, Karen, you see what's happening? Now it's three to one the other way. I've managed to get Dad and Roy on my side again."

Karen did not reply, but she still felt she was right. As far as she was concerned, the whole situation was much too serious to laugh about. If what Roy said were true, wouldn't the lady want to travel in front of them?

"Well," she managed. "I can't help having a strange feeling about it."

Mr. Tyler looked at the odometer. "According to the mileage, we have only a short distance left to go for today," he said. "Then we'll get a chance to eat and get some rest. That's probably what we all need."

Karen thought about it. Maybe her dad was right. After all, she had no proof that the lady was really following them. And even if she were, the mysterious woman was certainly doing no harm. Karen tried to put it out of her mind.

For a few miles there was silence in the car.

"Sure no neat scenery around this area," Dave said finally, breaking the silence.

Mr. Tyler glanced out the side window. "Not too much yet," he agreed. "But just wait until we get farther south."

"Hey," Roy interrupted excitedly. "There's a sign for the state campgrounds." He pointed to a big sign several hundred feet up the road. "That's where we're camping for the night, isn't it?"

Mr. Tyler nodded. "That's it, Roy. And to tell you the truth, I'm glad we're finally here." In a short while he drove the station wagon into the camping area.

Dave caught the sign of his dad's weariness.

"Dad, we could have helped you drive," he said.

Mr. Tyler shook his head.

"No," he said. "A learner's permit is not quite good enough for all this highway traveling," he laughed. "At least not for me."

"But Roy's got a regular license," Dave argued.

"Yeah," Roy agreed. "I'll take a turn anytime." He took out his billfold and pulled out his driver's license for proof.

"Maybe tomorrow." Mr. Tyler laughed. "Right now I have a good excuse for not being able to help set up the tents or fix the supper—I'm too tired."

"Neat trick, Dad," Dave laughed. "Come on, Roy, let's unload the wagon right away."

The boys began to pull out the camping equipment, and Karen went to get her suitcases out of the station wagon.

"Hey, you're not taking all three, are you?" Roy asked, hardly able to believe that Karen would consider such a thing.

"Yeah, Karen," her brother injected. "We're only staying here overnight, remember?"

Karen pushed the large piece of luggage back and pulled out her small overnight case. She laughed self-consciously. "I guess I wasn't thinking."

Turning from the station wagon, she looked up just as the familiar old camper pulled into the campground entrance.

"Coincidence?" she asked, looking at her brother.

24

"Is it a coincidence that she decided to follow us right into the camping area?"

Roy scratched his head, a bewildered look on his face.

"Boy, I'm really confused. I don't know what to make of it."

Karen looked directly at her brother.

"Let's see," she said, her voice thick with sarcasm. "This time you'll probably say she got sleepy the same time we did. Right?"

"Right," Dave replied casually. With that he turned to get more of the overnight equipment from the car.

"Here, Roy," he called. "Give me a hand, will you?"

Karen stared after them, a smile playing on the corners of her mouth.

"That Dave," she laughed.

In spite of the fact that Mr. Tyler had said he was too tired to help fix supper, he was the first one to unwrap the package of weiners and open a large can of beans. As he did, he looked at the food and then at his passengers.

"This is what we're having for supper, huh?" he asked without enthusiasm, looking at the two lonely items on the table.

"Oh, no," Dave said emphatically. "We've got more than that." He produced a large sack and pulled out a package of hot dog buns. "See, Dad. Bread. Lots of it."

Mr. Tyler shook his head slowly.

"It's been a long time since I've been camping," he complained good-naturedly. "So long, in fact, that I'd forgotten what the menus are like on these trips."

"It's not so bad, Mr. Tyler," Roy injected. "Just let your imagination run wild, and you'll think this is steak." He speared one of the hot dogs with a fork.

While the others were talking about hot dogs and steaks, Karen was thinking of ways to find out who, if anyone, was traveling with the lady in the mysterious camper.

Suddenly Karen's voice pierced above the laughter.

"Hey, I've got a terrific idea," she said, looking at her dad.

"You know how to make steaks out of hot dogs?" he asked.

Everyone laughed, including Karen.

"OK, Honey, what's your idea?" Mr. Tyler asked, going over to the old brick fireplace to start a fire.

Karen followed closely after her father.

"If that lady is really traveling all alone," she said, pointing toward the camper. "Then maybe—"

Dave looked at her in disbelief and interrupted her in mid-sentence.

"Not that again, Karen. Please."

But Karen Tyler was not going to be stopped.

"Well, I was just thinking, if she's alone, maybe she'd enjoy eating with us."

Mr. Tyler smiled and looked up at his daughter.

"Now, Karen, that's very thoughtful of you," he said. Then, turning to the boys, he asked, "Any objections?"

Dave wasn't too thrilled about the whole idea.

"You know what she's doing, don't you, Dad?" he retorted.

"I'm just asking if we should invite the lady to share our supper," Karen defended quickly.

Roy looked down at the food in the package and the can.

"You think she's the hot-dog-and-baked-beans type?" he asked.

"Well, if she had only milk and gelatin for lunch," Karen stated emphatically, "she'd probably even enjoy hot dogs and beans." She paused briefly. "Anyway, she'd probably be glad just to have a little company."

Dave shook his head in disbelief.

"And you'd be thrilled to see if you could find out who in that camper is holding her hostage. The big mystery—who drank the other carton of milk and ate the second serving of gelatin?"

Mr. Tyler stepped away from the fireplace. "Karen, in spite of your brother's objections, I think maybe you have a good idea," he said. "What do you say, Roy?"

Roy shrugged his shoulders.

"OK with me," he said. "There's plenty of food, that's for sure."

"And Dave?" Mr. Tyler said, walking over to his son.

Dave wasn't as enthusiastic as the others.

"First, you'd better make Karen promise that she won't go prying into all kinds of things that aren't her business," he said, looking over at his sister.

"OK, OK," Mr. Tyler said. "Karen, you can invite her to eat with us, but absolutely no quizzing. OK?"

Karen smiled broadly, a bright gleam in her eye.

"I wouldn't think of it," she said pleasantly. With that she turned to go and visit the mysterious lady in the camper.

27

Dave and Roy stared after her, but neither one said anything. Dave only shook his head in dismay.

"She's got something up her sleeve," he said finally, somewhat disturbed.

Karen heard what he said, turned and called back, "Just get another steak ready. We may have company for supper."

Chapter 4

A Baby With a Fever

For a long minute Karen stood beside the old camper and looked it over carefully. It certainly wasn't the latest model—Dave had been right about that. And if this lady weren't traveling alone, why would she be the only one who was driving? And why would she have such a beat-up old camper? Karen looked at it again. No wonder she wanted to stay close to the church station wagon. If anything went wrong, Karen's dad and the boys would probably be able to help her—or them.

Karen stepped up to the door and knocked timidly, then decided she would have to knock louder if the lady was going to hear it above the noises from the highway. Karen stood there waiting for what seemed to be an endless minute.

Finally, the door unlocked and opened ever so slightly.

"Yes, who is it?" called the woman.

Karen stepped back to allow the door to open wider.

"Oh!" said the woman, a look of surprise on her face. "You're the girl I met at the service station and the cafe, aren't you?"

Karen nodded, but for a moment she could not think of anything to say. It was true, the mysterious woman was not traveling alone. There in her arms was a young child.

"Oh," Karen said, surprise in her voice. "I didn't know you had a baby."

The woman smiled pleasantly. "Yes," she replied. "This is my Jeremy, but he's not feeling well today."

"We're fixing supper over there," Karen said, pointing to the place where her dad had parked the station wagon. "And we thought that since you are traveling alone, we'd invite you to come and eat with us."

The woman was obviously pleased but still nervous.

"Oh, thank you," she said sincerely. "That was really very kind of you. But I've got Jeremy's supper started, and I'm going to have to put him to bed as soon as he's eaten . . ." Her voice trailed off to almost nothing. "And I'm pretty tired from all the driving too."

Karen tried to steal a quick look into the camper to see if there were others inside, but she could not see beyond the entrance.

"Oh," Karen said simply in answer to the lady's reason for not joining them for supper. "Well, we just wanted you to know that you are welcome to eat with us. That is, if you like baked beans and weiners."

The young woman laughed heartily and then explained again that her young son was not feeling very well. "He seems to be running a fever."

Karen waved at the small child and then turned to leave.

"And thanks again," the lady called out and

then closed the camper door firmly. Karen heard the lock snap into place.

"I'm crushed," Roy said when Karen returned alone. "She wants to tag right behind us when we travel, but she doesn't want to share our steak with us."

Karen did not seem to pick up Roy's humor. Instead she walked over to her father.

"Well, I was right. She's not traveling alone, Dad," she said, still a little disturbed. "There's a baby in there too."

Mr. Tyler laughed. "Well, I guess we can rule out the ulcer theory as an explanation for the milk-and-gelatin diet. That's why she ordered two of everything."

The others laughed, but Karen wasn't amused.

"I tried to look in her camper," she reported. "It sure didn't seem very fancy."

Dave stared at his sister in disbelief.

"You couldn't tell that from the outside?" he asked disgustedly. "Man, that thing's ancient."

Mr. Tyler came to the woman's defense.

"Well, now, Dave, just because something is a little old, doesn't mean it's not in good condition. Look at the church station wagon we're using."

"Yeah, Dad," Dave laughed good-naturedly. "I have been looking at it. And so have all those people whizzing by and passing us." He stopped momentarily. "I think they really believe we and that lady are traveling together. Our vehicles seem to be of the same vintage."

Karen was not interested in either the age of the vehicles or their condition. Her thoughts were still on the baby.

"He's not feeling well," she said unconsciously,

31

forgetting for the moment that she had not even mentioned the child's name.

"Who's not feeling well?" Roy asked inquisitively.

"Jeremy," she said. "That's the baby's name."

"Nice name," her father said casually.

"And I suppose you'll want to travel in her camper the rest of the way so you can babysit for her," Dave injected. "And find out what's going on."

Karen took a deep breath, ignoring Dave's comment. "I'll bet the lady would appreciate it," she countered. "She said Jeremy isn't feeling well. He's running a fever."

"Well," Mr. Tyler laughed, going over to check on the supper. "I think you'd better plan to travel with us. Mrs. Black needs you for Bible school, and there'll be plenty of children there you can take care of."

After that Mr. Tyler led the small group in prayer, asking God's blessing on the food, their travels, their ministry in Arizona and finally praying for the needs of the lady and her baby. When he finished, Roy and Dave immediately stuck their forks into the hot dogs, forgetting their back-home manners.

"Now, pretend this is steak," Roy insisted, putting a hot dog on Karen's plate.

But Karen Tyler wasn't hungry for either hot dogs or steak. For some reason, there seemed to be a hard lump in the pit of her stomach. She couldn't get the lady in the camper out of her mind. Something seemed wrong, but she couldn't think of what it was.

32

Why did she have such an uneasy feeling about everything? Was it like Dave said—she just made too much out of everything? Suddenly she found herself offering up another prayer for the mysterious woman and her baby. She stopped. She was praying—something she didn't do too often anymore. Strange how she had allowed herself to get away from that habit.

Maybe that was it: Prayer had become a habit to her, and just about the only time she prayed was when things were beyond her own ability to change. That was wrong, she knew that. But for some reason that's the way her Christian life had been lately.

As she thought about it, she was very much ashamed.

Chapter 5

Campground Devotions

Even though Roy Sparton and Dave Tyler ate heartily, Karen hardly touched her supper. She never had been able to eat when she was upset, and for some unexplainable reason, she was upset about Jeremy.

"What's the matter?" Roy teased. "You don't like beans and hot dogs?"

Before Karen could answer, Dave spoke up, forgetting for the moment his father's earlier warnings.

"She's busy plotting the next chapter in the life of Mrs. Tagalong."

As he spoke his voice took on a hollow, spooky sound.

Karen said nothing. Instead she made a gallant effort to take another bite of her hot dog.

Her father quickly changed the subject of conversation.

"Well," he said, pushing away an empty paper plate. "Camping has at least one plus. There aren't any dishes to clean up."

"Yeah," Roy said. "But we do have to put up the tents and drag out the bedrolls."

"That's right," Mr. Tyler said pleasantly. "I'll help Karen with hers, and you guys put up the other one."

Dave looked over at his sister. "It must be neat to

be the weaker sex," he teased, "especially on a camping trip." He laughed as he spoke, indicating that he was really only teasing.

"Hey," Roy defended. "Don't bother her. Can't you see she's busy putting the dishes in the dishwasher?"

Karen smiled as she cleared away the paper plates from the table and put them in the park garbage container. Roy always seemed to come to her defense when he sensed that Dave was going a little too far with his teasing. Good old Roy; he was a real friend.

"I wish it was this easy at home," she said, rolling up the paper table covering and putting it with the garbage.

Darkness was beginning to fall, and Mr. Tyler suggested that everyone turn in right away so they could get up and get an early start.

"What's early?" Dave asked, knowing full well that his father's idea of "early" was quite different from his own. Whenever the family took a trip, they always left at the first glimpse of daylight.

Mr. Tyler put his hand on his son's shoulder.

"How's 5:00 a.m. sound?"

"Five a.m.?" a chorus of voices exploded together.

"Well," Mr. Tyler laughed. "Maybe we won't have to start quite that early, but if we're going to make the rest of the trip in one day, we're going to have to get an early start."

"Are we going to have devotions before we sack out?" Dave asked.

"Yes, we certainly are," Mr. Tyler replied. He looked up at the already darkening sky. "It's a little dark to read," he said, "so why don't we each

35

quote a favorite Scripture verse and share something of God's goodness to us. Then we'll have prayer."

Roy started. "I like the verse in Psalm 86:12: 'I will praise thee, O Lord my God, with all my heart: and I will glorify thy name for evermore.' " He paused. "I just memorized that one this week."

Mr. Tyler nodded. "Well, that's certainly a good one, Roy." He stopped momentarily. When he spoke again, there was a break in his voice. "That's my prayer too," he said. "That I'll always glorify the Lord in everything I do."

There was a brief silence before Karen spoke up.

"My verse is in the Psalms too," she said. " 'Create in me a clean heart, O God; and renew a right spirit within me.' That's Psalm 51:10."

"Another wonderful verse," Mr. Tyler admitted. "And another prayer that I pray regularly. You know, it's so easy to become soiled with the things of this world, so we do need to pray that God will give us clean hearts and right spirits, don't we?"

There was another short silence, and then Dave began.

"I'm trying to decide which verse to give," he said as the others turned to look at him.

"Whichever one seems to mean something special to you right now," Mr. Tyler said, helping him along.

"Is there one that says, 'Thou shalt not pick on thy sister'?" Karen suggested pleasantly.

Everyone laughed heartily, sharing in the good-natured humor.

Finally Dave spoke. "No, the verses I learned don't say anything about a sister." He paused. "It's about parents. I've been trying to memorize the sixth chapter of Ephesians," he confessed. "Pastor Don suggested that in our youth meeting last week."

"Oh, yeah," Roy confessed. "I forgot all about that."

Dave continued. "It starts, 'Children, obey your parents in the Lord: for this is right. Honour thy father and mother; which is the first commandment with promise; that it may be well with thee, and thou mayest live long on the earth.' " He stopped. "That's all I've memorized so far."

"Well, I'd say that was pretty good," Mr. Tyler said. "Now, let me give you one of my favorite verses, and then we'll pray."

Mr. Tyler paused for a long minute, obviously thinking about the verse he was about to quote. "I love this one," he said. There was strong emotion in his voice. " 'Delight thyself also in the Lord; and he shall give thee the desires of thine heart'— Psalm 37:4."

Karen had a question.

"Dad," she said seriously. "Does that mean that if we're delightful or happy Christians, God will give us anything we desire?"

Mr. Tyler was quiet. "I suppose some people would look at it that way," he said finally. "But I think a better way to think about it is that a person who is really and truly committed to the Lord will ask God to direct him even in his desires so that they will be pleasing to the Lord. Then our desires will be God's desires, and it'll be easy for God to give us the desires of our hearts."

The others let that message sink into their thoughts too. Finally they had a time of silent prayer before Mr. Tyler led them aloud. He asked

God to give them a good night's rest so they would be able to take the long, tiring trip the next day. He prayed for Mrs. Tyler and his young son, Teddy, back home in Trendale. Once more he remembered the lady that Dave had pegged "Mrs. Tagalong." Then with very little further conversation, each of them headed for his own sleeping bag.

For a long time Karen lay in her tent thinking about all the things that had taken place during the day. Strange what an important part this mysterious woman had seemed to play in the activities of their day. Maybe Dave was right when he said that Karen had made too much of the whole incident. After all, it was very possible that the woman just happened to be traveling the same route to Arizona. And like Roy said, she no doubt felt a certain amount of security in traveling behind the church station wagon. She had probably even seen them bow for prayer in the cafe and felt that this was a group she could trust. And the reason the camper had still been in the cafe parking lot when they had finished their noon meal was obvious too. After all, the lady had a baby, and she would have to feed the child before she could start traveling again. Yes, everything was falling into place. She should have thought of all this earlier. If she had, she would not have had to tolerate so much of Dave's teasing and her own distress.

In spite of the hot temperature during the day, the evening produced a cool, pleasant breeze, very conducive to outdoor sleeping. Everything in the other tent was quiet. Her father and the boys had probably gone to sleep right away. They weren't as concerned about Jeremy or his mother as she was.

Karen reached for the transistor radio she had insisted on taking along. Now she was glad; maybe some soft music would help her to relax and get to sleep more easily. She dialed until she found the type of music she wanted.

Karen was just beginning to drift off to sleep when a newscast came on. But she hardly heard it. The announcer was saying something about a child who had meningitis. Karen tried to listen to the entire report, but her eyelids became heavy, and soon she was fast asleep.

From that moment Karen Tyler heard nothing until her father called to her.

"It's not morning, is it?" she asked, looking out at the sun-filled sky and hoping against hope that her father would tell her she could sleep for another hour.

"Yes, it is," her father replied instead. "The boys already have the fire going for breakfast."

Sleepily she unzipped her sleeping bag and crawled out of the tent. She stretched lazily and looked around the campground. Something looked different than it had when she went to bed. She wondered what it was. Suddenly she knew! The camper! The mysterious old camper was gone!

Chapter 6

The Disappearing Camper

Dave, too, noticed that the camper was missing.

"Well, Karen," he called mockingly. "That takes care of the mystery of the tagalong camper. Your friend took off without us."

"I didn't hear her leave," Roy confessed. "Did you?"

Karen shook her head. "No," she admitted. "Once I got to sleep, I guess I slept too soundly to hear anything."

"I wonder why she left before we did?" Roy asked the question that was on Karen's mind. "She seemed to wait for us all day yesterday."

Mr. Tyler picked up the package of bacon and started to walk over to the fireplace with it. He stopped suddenly.

"Well, maybe we should take that as a positive sign," he smiled. "If the lady was a bit frightened about traveling yesterday, evidently she feels more secure now and . . ."

A patrol car drove into the camping area, and Mr. Tyler turned to see where it was going.

"Here, Mr. Tyler," Roy said. "I'll put that bacon on." He took the package from Karen's father and began to place the slices in a skillet.

"Looks like he's stopping here," Dave said to his father, both of them watching as the officer got out of his car.

"Good morning," Mr. Tyler called.

The officer smiled broadly. "Say, just in time for breakfast," he said. "Too bad I've already eaten."

"You're welcome to share our food with us," Mr. Tyler replied. "Or even have a cup of coffee."

The officer shook his head.

"No. I've had my breakfast, and it's too early for a coffee break, thank you." He looked around as though he was scanning the area. "I just stopped to see if anyone here had seen a young woman and a little boy come into this campground."

"A young woman and a child?" Mr. Tyler repeated.

Karen looked at her dad, wondering if he was going to tell the officer about Jeremy and his mother.

"Has she done something?" Dave asked, taking a step or two closer to the uniformed man.

"No," the officer laughed. "Actually, it's the child we're after."

Roy finished putting the bacon into the pan and came over to join the others. He scratched his head. "Well, it sure can't be the little guy who's done something." He laughed loudly.

The look on the policeman's face changed and became very serious. "If we don't find that child soon, he could die," he said soberly.

"What's the problem?" Mr. Tyler asked, concern in his voice.

"The youngster has meningitis."

"Meningitis?" Roy called out. "That's a bad disease, isn't it?"

The officer nodded. "Very bad and very infectious."

"Oh," Karen called out when she heard the

41

officer's report. "I heard something about it on the radio last night right after I went to bed. But I fell asleep during the report. I didn't know it was Jeremy."

"Jeremy?" the policeman asked. "You know the child?"

Mr. Tyler put his arm around Karen's shoulder.

"Not really," he said. "My daughter just met a lady and a little boy last night—right here in the campgrounds."

"Was he all right?" the policeman asked.

Karen began to shiver as she spoke.

"I think so," she said, trying to control her quavering voice. She stopped. "No," she said, correcting herself. "He wasn't feeling too well. His mother said he was running a fever."

Mr. Tyler looked down at his daughter. He held her more tightly.

"Now we don't know that it's Jeremy this officer is looking for, Karen," he said, trying to make his voice convincing enough to comfort her. "This could be some other little boy."

The police officer pulled out a small black book.

"Can you give me a description of the child?" he asked, looking directly at Karen.

She wasn't sure. "I hardly saw him," she confessed. "His mother was holding him."

"Holding him?" the officer asked. "You mean carrying him as if he was very sick?"

She nodded. "He was sick," she insisted.

The officer continued to probe.

"And what about the mother? Did you see her?" he asked.

Karen nodded again.

"Describe her," the uniformed man said bluntly.

"She's sort of tall, black hair, brown eyes." Karen stopped. "I guess that's all I know."

"You don't have her name?" the officer insisted.

Karen shook her head. "I didn't ask her any questions." She looked up at her brother briefly. If only Dave had not insisted that she should not quiz the lady, maybe she could be of more help now. But even as these thoughts plagued her, she knew it was not at all her brother's fault.

As they talked, a call came over the radio in the officer's car. The man excused himself and went over to take it. The others followed.

"Discontinue the search for the little child with meningitis," the dispatch operator said. "The child was located and is now in isolation at Central Avenue Hospital in Claremont. Treatment has been started."

The police officer took off his hat and wiped the perspiration from his forehead.

"Well, that's good news," he smiled. "They don't all turn out that way."

He put his hat back on his head and turned to leave.

"Where's Claremont?" Roy called after him.

"Claremont?" He stopped for a moment to think. "Straight north about 30 miles," he said as he opened the door to his vehicle. Karen was sure Roy was thinking the same thing she was thinking. They would have to go to the hospital to see if the sick boy was Jeremy and to try to be of help to his mother. She must be frantic, having to take her son to a strange hospital.

The police officer broke into her thoughts.

"Well, you folks have a good day now," he said. He started his car and drove away.

43

Karen watched until he was completely out of sight.

"That's why she left without us," Karen said as though they had just been discussing the lady's early departure.

"Yeah," Roy added. "I'll bet her baby got sick— or sicker—during the night, and she had to take him to the hospital."

"Don't you think we ought to go to Claremont and check on her?" Karen asked, looking pleadingly at her father.

"That's way out of our way," Dave called, holding up a shriveled piece of burned bacon. "We're getting a late start as it is."

"But Dad," Karen insisted, still talking with her father. "We prayed that the Lord would help us to do whatever we were supposed to do to help her. Isn't this our chance?"

Mr. Tyler nodded. "Yes, Karen, I was thinking the same thing. But Dave has a point too. It's going to bring us into camp very late. If we go to Claremont, we'd better find a phone first and call Mrs. Black and explain."

"Anyone for super, well-done bacon?" Dave called, holding up another piece of charred meat.

Roy sat down at the table and looked at their breakfast. Then he turned and faced Karen and Dave's father.

"I'll tell you what, Mr. Tyler, you'd better add an extra half hour to whatever time you decide to tell Mrs. Black," he said. "I have a feeling we're going to need to make a breakfast stop too."

They all ate quickly and then started loading the car. Karen got her bedroll and overnight case and put them into the station wagon. She watched

44

as her father took down her tent and helped the boys get the camping gear back in the car. Then, opening the car door, she got in. As she did, she prayed aloud, "Please, Lord, help Jeremy to be all right. Please."

With tears in her eyes, she sat back, waiting for the others to get in, ready for what would be a long ride to Claremont.

Chapter 7

"Jeremy Isn't Here"

The 30 miles between the state campgrounds and Claremont seemed endless, almost as long as the entire trip had seemed the day before. Even Dave became genuinely concerned about the baby. And he hadn't even seen him.

"I'm sure glad you got in touch with Mrs. Black, Dad," Dave said after his father returned from the phone booth.

"Yes, she was very understanding," said Mr. Tyler. "She has a daughter with a child too. So she understood fully."

"How are you going to find the hospital once you get into Claremont?" Roy asked. "Or did the policeman tell you where it was?"

"Well, I assume it's on Central Avenue," said Mr. Tyler.

"Do you know where Central Avenue is?" Karen questioned.

Mr. Tyler shook his head. "No, actually I don't. But most towns have signs right on the main highways pointing in the direction of the hospital."

That information seemed to satisfy Karen, at least for the moment.

"You know what I can't understand?" Roy injected when there seemed to be a lull in the conversation.

Dave turned to face him. "What's that?"

"How could a mother start out on a long trip when she knew her little baby was sick?"

Dave shrugged. "I can't figure that out either," he admitted. "And she must have known if the baby had a fever."

This bothered Karen too. The lady had seemed so sincere and so thoughtful about everything. How could she be so neglectful about this? Unless there was someone else telling her what to do.

Mr. Tyler entered the conversation again.

"Of course, she might have had her baby checked before she left and been told that it wasn't serious," he said in the woman's defense. "Maybe the meningitis was discovered in some tests or something."

"Yeah," Karen agreed. That had to be it. Someone had no doubt checked it.

As Mr. Tyler reached the Claremont city limits, everyone in the station wagon began looking for a hospital sign. There it was, just as Mr. Tyler had said it would be.

From force of habit Karen turned and looked through the back window. For most of the trip the old camper had been following them, and it almost seemed as though it should be right behind them now. But of course, it wouldn't be, not with little Jeremy sick in the hospital.

"What are meningitis treatments like?" Karen asked when they neared the street where the hospital was located.

"I'm not sure," her father replied. "I know it's a very serious disease, and . . ." His voice faded.

"Poor Jeremy," Karen said, thinking about the little boy she had seen ever so briefly.

47

"There's the hospital," Dave said, pointing to a big building around the corner.

Mr. Tyler turned into the parking area and pulled into the nearest empty stall.

"Maybe we should wait here for you to check it out first," Roy said, sure they would be in the way if they all went in.

"No," Karen objected. "I want to go with you. After all, I'm the only one who met the lady."

Mr. Tyler nodded his approval. "OK," he said. Then, turning to the boys, he said, "One of us will come back to report to you. OK?"

Roy nodded. "And we'll be praying that everything turns out OK."

Mr. Tyler smiled broadly.

"Well, you know what the Scripture verse you quoted last night said—that everything should be done to glorify the Lord. That's still true, you know."

Karen found it difficult to wait while her father talked to Dave and Roy. In one way she wanted to get into the hospital and see Jeremy's mother, whatever her name was. In another way, she was frightened. Maybe the news would not be good. Maybe there had been too long a delay between the onset of the disease and the time treatment began.

Once inside the building, Karen began to feel trembly. Her dad seemed to sense it.

" 'All things work together for good to them that love God, to them who are the called according to his purpose,' " her father repeated aloud. "We've got to believe that, Karen." He squeezed her hand.

Karen believed it. Or at least she felt she did. She knew her father was right. And there was no question in her mind that the Bible was right. But right now she was afraid—afraid of the consequences of their investigation. Suddenly she wished she had gotten to know the lady better. Maybe they could have talked more and shared some of these problems. If they had, Jeremy might have gotten here sooner.

Mr. Tyler opened a second glass door and waited for Karen to go in first. As they stepped up to the receptionist's desk, they waited for her to finish her telephone conversation. She looked up at them.

"Yes," she smiled pleasantly. "May I help you?"

"Yes," Mr. Tyler acknowledged. "Could you tell me if a lady brought a young child in here during the night or this morning—"

"And what is the patient's last name?" the girl interrupted before Karen's father had finished.

"We don't know the last name," Karen interrupted. "We just met this lady while—"

Mr. Tyler put his hand on Karen's shoulder.

"Honey, let me take care of this, please?" He turned again to the receptionist. "I'm sorry, my daughter is quite concerned. Please forgive her."

The receptionist shot a friendly smile toward Karen.

"I understand. I see that all day long."

Mr. Tyler began again to explain the situation.

"The child is a boy—we don't know his exact age. His first name is Jeremy." He tried to speak calmly, but there was a definite quiver in his voice.

"I'm sorry, Sir," the girl said softly. "I'm not at liberty to give out any information unless you are part of the family."

"Then they're here?" Karen shot back without thinking. "Jeremy and his mother are here?"

The receptionist smiled at her again.

"Honey," she said, a little more firmly than before. "I not only don't know who you're talking about, but I can't tell you anything about any of the patients here."

"We believe the child may have meningitis," Mr. Tyler explained.

"Meningitis?" the receptionist asked, a new concern in her voice.

"Yes, did you admit someone like that?"

"I'm sorry," the girl said again. "Let me call Admissions and see if they know anything about it." She dialed the number. "Jeremy?" she asked while waiting.

Karen nodded.

Mr. Tyler stepped back and took hold of Karen's arm as he did. "We'll soon know," he assured her.

"Why can't they tell us something?" Karen asked almost angrily.

"Well, Honey, they're not at liberty to give out information to just anyone."

Karen Tyler was not satisfied with that answer. "But the policeman said they were here, remember?"

As they talked, the girl behind the desk called to them.

"I just talked to Admissions," she said kindly, "and they say no one by the name of Jeremy was admitted either last night or this morning. I'm sorry."

"Are you sure?" Karen snapped.

"I can only tell you what Admissions said," the receptionist answered, slightly disturbed. "I'm sorry."

Mr. Tyler thanked the receptionist and took his

daughter's hand and led her through the hospital lobby.

"Well, Honey," he said sympathetically. "They must have given us the wrong hospital. Jeremy isn't here."

Karen Tyler burst into uncontrollable sobs.

Chapter 8

"Do You Have a Minute?"

Mr. Tyler led his teenage daughter toward the exit of the Central Avenue Hospital.

"Well," he said gently, keen disappointment in his voice, "we tried."

But Karen Tyler was not satisfied.

"Daddy," she said, her voice breaking as she spoke, "we've got to find them." She stopped long enough to regain her composure. "Meningitis is serious; we've got to find Jeremy."

Mr. Tyler shook his head in despair.

"Honey," he said almost frantically, "he's not here. Didn't you hear the receptionist tell us that no one has been admitted to this hospital recently by the name of Jeremy?"

Karen could not respond. Reluctantly she allowed herself to be led through the lobby toward the outside door.

"Sir," a call came from the opposite direction of the exit. "Please, Sir, do you have a minute?"

Karen and her father turned quickly at the sound of the caller's voice. Mr. Tyler stepped back into the large lobby, and Karen followed.

"Excuse me," the lady said when they came together. Karen noticed that her eyes were red and swollen—it was evident that she had been crying.

"Yes?" Mr. Tyler replied, surprise in his eyes as well as his voice. "Did you want to talk to us?"

"Please," the lady repeated. She stopped to dab at her eyes. "I know what you are going through," she said brokenly.

Karen wasn't sure what the lady was talking about, but she listened with intense interest.

"You see," she began again, "my little boy is in here with meningitis too."

"Meningitis?" Karen asked almost fearfully. "Your little boy has meningitis? When did he get sick?"

"Yesterday," the lady replied. She took a deep breath and then looked around for a place to sit down. "Can we go over here?" she asked, pointing to the opposite side of the room. Mr. Tyler nodded. He and Karen followed her in spite of the fact that they did not feel they should take the time. After all, there was still Jeremy and his mother to look for and several hours of traveling besides.

The threesome sat down, and for a moment, nobody seemed to know what to say.

"I'm sorry about your little boy," Mr. Tyler said finally, breaking the silence. "Is he getting along all right?"

The lady nodded.

"I think so," she said brokenly. "He's in isolation, and they're giving him medication."

She paused for a long time. Neither Karen nor her father said anything, allowing the woman to regain her composure.

"We were driving to my mother's place," the lady spoke haltingly. "Billy said he didn't feel well, but the doctor had said it was just a virus. I had him there yesterday."

Karen looked into the woman's face.

"Didn't he know it was meningitis?"

The woman shook her head. "He ran some tests and said he'd get in touch if it was anything serious." She paused briefly. "Then he got so sick. I just drove directly to the hospital. That's when I found out the police had been alerted to look for us."

"But they think you got here in time, don't they? He's going to be all right now, isn't he?" Karen asked, feeling great sympathy for the distraught mother.

"I hope so." She stopped, facing Mr. Tyler. "That's why I wanted to talk to you about your little friend. I heard you asking about a little boy, and I saw the disappointment on your girl's face when they said he wasn't in this hospital. I just had to tell you that it's a terrible experience, but if he's in a hospital, they'll pull him through."

Mr. Tyler nodded. "Well, thank you. That's very kind of you," he said softly. "Actually, we don't know this little boy we're looking for. My daughter just met him yesterday. He and his mother were traveling and—"

"Hey, Dad," Karen broke in with sudden light on her face. "Maybe Jeremy isn't the baby who has meningitis at all. It was probably this lady's little boy that the policeman was looking for at the campground this morning."

Mr. Tyler nodded. "That could be."

"They were even checking campgrounds for us?" the lady asked.

Karen nodded. "But then they reported that you were already here."

"And what about your little friend?" the lady asked. "You're not sure he was sick like Billy?"

"No, not really," Mr. Tyler answered and then

54

went on to explain how the woman in the camper had parked near them at the campgrounds.

"My daughter went to invite her to have supper with us. And that's when she saw the little child. He was running a fever, and—"

Karen interrupted.

"So when we heard about the sick baby, I thought it just had to be Jeremy. But I guess it must have been your Billy."

Her enthusiasm was of no comfort to the distraught woman.

"I almost wish it had been your little friend," she confessed honestly. Then she stopped abruptly. "No, I wouldn't want to wish this on anyone else."

Mr. Tyler looked at his watch.

"Well, we still have a long trip left for today," he said apologetically. "So I think we'll have to be on our way."

The woman understood. "Oh, sure," she said, an unbidden tear trickling down her face. "I'm sorry I delayed you. I just thought maybe I could make you feel better."

"Oh, I'm sorry," Mr. Tyler said, realizing that the woman had misinterpreted his words. "I am glad you stopped us. And I certainly will be praying for your little son."

With only a few more words, Mr. Tyler and Karen started for the door for the second time. Suddenly Mr. Tyler stopped.

"This isn't right," he said aloud. "I can't leave that poor woman sitting there without telling her that the Lord can help her. You go ahead to the car. I'll be right back."

Karen looked up at her dad, a pleading look in her eyes.

"Can't I go along?" she begged.

He nodded.

"If you'd like," he said. "I want to go back and have prayer with her and talk with her about the Lord."

Once again Karen and her father returned to the hospital lobby. The lady was still sitting in the same chair, her face buried in her hands.

Karen knelt down beside her.

"Ma'am," she said softly. "We came back. We didn't want you to sit here all alone, and . . ." She stopped, not knowing what else to say.

Mr. Tyler noted her hesitancy and sat down in a chair across from them.

"I wanted to have prayer with you before we left," he began. "That is, if you have no objections."

"Objections? No, of course not." She stopped and looked squarely into Mr. Tyler's face. "Are you a minister?"

"No," he replied pleasantly. "But I'm a Christian. And I felt that I wanted to pray with you about your son. Would that be all right?"

"That would be nice," the lady managed, taking another tissue from her purse.

Karen and her father bowed their heads, and Mr. Tyler began to ask the Lord to be with the lady they had just met. He prayed for her son and asked God to restore him to health and strength if it was His will. He paused, and as he did, he heard the young lady's sobs.

"I wish I could pray," she said, even before he had finished. "I wish I could talk to the Almighty like you do. But I can't."

Mr. Tyler looked directly into the face of the woman seated across from him.

"Why not?" he asked tenderly. "Why do you feel you can't talk to God?"

She shook her head.

"Because He won't listen to me," she said flatly.

Karen could stand it no longer.

"But God always listens when people pray," she said emphatically.

"Not to me, He wouldn't," the woman insisted. "I-I . . . chucked all my religion when I was in college," she finally confessed. "The little I had."

"But praying to God isn't dependent on the amount of religion we have," Mr. Tyler said, choosing his words carefully. "And to tell you the truth, God isn't particularly interested in anyone's religion."

The woman looked up, surprise written all over her face.

"You've got to be kidding!" she said in disbelief. "If God isn't interested in religion, then who is?"

Mr. Tyler sat quietly for a moment. Karen knew that he was forming his words carefully before speaking.

"Ma'am," he said and then stopped. "I'm sorry. I haven't even asked you your name."

She wiped at her eyes once more. "Julie Swartz," she said simply.

"Well, Mrs. Swartz," Mr. Tyler began again. "Would you let me tell you how you can talk to God about your little boy and know for a fact that He'll hear your prayers?"

She nodded silently.

"God knows our hearts," Mr. Tyler began quietly. "He knows what we're thinking even before the words are expressed. And He loves us dearly."

She shook her head again.

"Not me. He can't love me," she repeated. "Not the way I've ignored Him."

"But He does love you," Mr. Tyler insisted. There was a note of sincere kindness in his statement. "Have you heard of John 3:16?" he asked.

The woman nodded. "Yeah, I guess everybody has."

"Do you know what it says?" Mr. Tyler continued.

The woman dabbed at her eyes again. "Not really, I guess."

Karen looked up at her father, her eyes asking for permission to say something.

"I'll say it, Daddy," she said and then softly began quoting her favorite verse.

" 'For God so loved the world,' " Karen said. "That's you. 'That he gave his only begotten Son'—that's Jesus. 'That whosoever—' "

"That's me," the lady interrupted.

"Yes," Karen continued more enthusiastically. " 'That whosoever believeth in him'—that's Jesus— 'should not perish, but have everlasting life.' "

"And that's love," Mr. Tyler finished. "God's love."

The woman caught another tear rolling down her cheek. There was a new look of interest on her face.

"That's beautiful," she said. "I knew part of that verse, but I could never have said it."

"Well, we wanted to give you that verse so that you would understand how much God loves you," Mr. Tyler smiled. "He does, you know, and because of His great love, He sent His Son, Jesus, to die for Julie Swartz. Did you know that?"

She was silent for a moment. "This makes me think of my childhood," she confessed. "My grandmother used to talk to me about the Bible. But I haven't thought much about it since."

"Well," Mr. Tyler said kindly. "It's not so much what you did with those days that is important to you right now. It's what you do with today." He paused again. "Mrs. Swartz," he said evenly. "Could I read some other verses to you from the Bible?"

She nodded. "Sure."

Mr. Tyler reached into his shirt pocket and pulled out a New Testament.

"Here, in Romans 3," he said, turning the pages of his Testament, "it tells us that this world is full of sin." He looked up at Mrs. Swartz as he spoke. "And, of course, we're part of the world, and all of us have sinned. In fact, verse 23 says, 'All have sinned, and come short of the glory of God.' That includes Karen, me, you—everyone."

The woman nodded again. "That's for sure," she said, taking a deep breath as she spoke.

"Well, you've just taken the first step toward changing things in your life," Mr. Tyler said, smiling. "You see, when we confess that we are sinners, then God can do something for us."

"Like what?" she questioned, doubt in her voice.

"Like forgive our sins," Mr. Tyler replied. "Now, you said you were a sinner," he repeated. "Is that right?"

"I sure am," Julie Swartz admitted.

"And are you ready to let God take away your sins and forgive you and make you a new person?" Mr. Tyler asked.

There was no hesitation.

"I would if I knew how," she replied quickly.

"Here," Mr. Tyler said, turning the pages of his Testament again, "let me read another verse." With that he turned to Romans 6:23. " 'The wages of sin is death; but the gift of God is eternal life through Jesus Christ our Lord.' "

Mrs. Swartz shook her head.

"I'm afraid I don't know what all that means," she confessed.

"Then let me explain," Mr. Tyler said simply. "God says that if we confess that we are sinners, and you've done that, that He will forgive our sins and give us eternal life. Those who refuse will receive the wages of sin, which is death." He paused. "But those who believe receive eternal life," he repeated carefully.

"And you think God will forgive all my sins?" the woman asked, a new spark of interest in both her voice and eyes.

"I know He will," Mr. Tyler assured her. "He did it for me and for Karen and for hundreds of others."

There was a long silence.

"I wish ..." the woman stopped. "I wish I'd done something like this years ago."

Mr. Tyler closed his New Testament and held it between his hands.

"It's today that counts, Mrs. Swartz," he said firmly. "God will forgive all your past, whatever is involved."

She looked up at him as though he must have understood what kind of life she had lived.

"God will forgive everything?" she asked, disbelief in her voice.

"Everything," Mr. Tyler repeated. "Won't you

come to Christ now and tell Him you want for-
giveness?"

There was another long, painful silence. Finally
the woman broke down in a sob.

"Oh, yes, Sir," she confessed. "That's exactly
what I want."

Karen put her arm around the sobbing woman
and waited for her father to pray aloud.

Chapter 9

The Long Wait

Dave and Roy were becoming restless while they waited in the church-owned station wagon.

"Man, I can't think of anything that should take this long," Roy complained.

Dave did not agree.

"That's because you don't know Karen," he said. "When she wants something, she stays with it, no matter how long it takes."

"But what could they be doing in there all this time?" Roy probed. "If they found that baby and his mother, there wouldn't be much to do, except tell her we were all praying for her."

Dave agreed. "And if they didn't find them, then Dad and Karen should have been out long ago."

Roy turned again and looked out of the car window.

"Still no sign of them," he said, a bit disgruntled by the long wait.

"You think we ought to go in and check things out?" Dave asked, his hand already on the door handle.

Roy shrugged.

"Would you know where to look?" he asked.

"Well, we'd have time to check over the whole hospital and still not take as long as Dad and Karen have taken," Dave said, opening the door and stepping out.

Roy followed him.

"Where'll we start?" he asked, looking around the grounds.

"Well, they sure aren't outside," Dave said, "or we'd see them. I think they went in this center door," he said, pointing to what seemed to be the main entrance. "I'm for trying it anyway."

Roy did not argue. "I wonder if they page visitors like they page doctors," he said, laughing.

Dave laughed too. "Man, if we paged them, Karen would never forgive us."

"It'd make her seem awfully important, wouldn't it?" Roy suggested.

"It'd also make her feel very silly," Dave countered. "And that's the part that would make her boil."

The boys stepped into the hospital lobby. Quickly they scanned the area.

"There's the information desk," Dave said. "Let's start there."

The boys walked toward the reception area, but before they got there, Dave stopped.

"Hey," he whispered. "I hear Dad's voice."

"You do?" Roy questioned.

"Yeah, I'm sure I heard him praying," Dave insisted.

They looked around and soon spotted Mr. Tyler and Karen with the young woman. Mr. Tyler had a New Testament clenched between his hands and was praying aloud.

"Hey," Roy said. "They must have found her." He looked around the small room. "You don't suppose something happened to Jeremy and your Dad and Karen are trying to . . ." He stopped before saying what he was really thinking.

63

Dave shook his head.

"I don't know," he replied. "But I feel like a dummy for wondering what they were doing in here all the time."

"Yeah," Roy agreed. "Me too. We should have known your dad would be talking with her about the Lord."

Dave signaled his friend.

"Let's get out of here. It sort of seems like sacred ground or something."

"Yeah," Roy agreed. "Let's get back in the car and wait like we should have done in the first place."

*　　*　　*

In the hospital waiting area, Mr. Tyler was just finishing his prayer.

"And we thank You for what You've done for Mrs. Swartz," he prayed tenderly. "We continue to ask for Your perfect and wonderful will to be done in Billy's life. And it's in Jesus name that we pray, with thanksgiving. Amen."

As Karen and her father rose to leave for the second time, Julie Swartz stretched out her hand to Mr. Tyler.

"Oh, thank you, thank you," she said over and over again. "To think it had to take this to get me on right terms with God."

Mr. Tyler smiled. "God works in mysterious ways," he replied.

Karen, too, tried to shake the lady's hand, but Mrs. Swartz threw her arms around the Tyler girl.

"Do you know," she said appreciatively, "that if you hadn't cared enough for that other mother and baby to come to the hospital, I wouldn't be God's child now?"

Karen thought about that. Suddenly she remembered the times when she, like Mrs. Swartz, had not been willing to consider God—until something seemingly tragic happened. Her mind went back to a specific night when she had felt so close to God. She remembered kneeling beside her bed and promising Him that she would live devotedly for Christ, that she would witness when He gave her the opportunities and that her Bible reading and prayer time would become an important part of her life. She had almost forgotten that promise—until now. Maybe God allowed this whole incident not only for Julie Swartz but also for Karen Tyler. She thought about that for a long while.

"Well, Honey," her father was saying. "We still have many miles to go before we get to the Bible camp."

She turned and put her arms around Mrs. Swartz again. Strange that the new convert almost seemed like a close friend or a member of the family. But then, she was. They were both members of God's family, weren't they?

"I'm sure Roy and Dave are wondering what took us so long," Mr. Tyler said as they left the hospital and walked across the parking lot to the car.

"I guess we have been gone a long time," Karen said, looking at her watch. "But it sure was worth it, wasn't it, Dad?"

Mr. Tyler nodded his answer. Finally he spoke. "It sure was."

At the car Karen and her father were bombarded with questions the minute they got in.

65

"How's Jeremy?" Roy asked. "Is he going to be OK?"

But before either Karen or her dad could give an answer, Dave interrupted.

"We thought it was taking such a long time that we decided to go in and see what was going on. We saw you praying with Jeremy's mother, and—"

Mr. Tyler held up his hand to get Dave's attention.

"That wasn't Jeremy's mother," Karen stated before her father could say anything. "That was Mrs. Swartz."

Dave scratched his head. "Who's Mrs. Swartz?"

"That's what I was going to tell you," Mr. Tyler said, fastening the seat belt and starting the car. He said no more before he drove out of the parking area and onto the street.

But Karen couldn't wait.

"We asked for Jeremy when we went to the receptionist's desk," she began. "And they checked all the records and told us nobody by that name had been admitted recently into the hospital."

"Then where is he?" Dave asked, concern in his voice.

"We still don't know," Karen answered soberly.

"How'd you get to talking to this Mrs. Swartz?" Roy wanted to know.

This time it was Mr. Tyler's turn.

"That's something only God could have worked out," he said jubilantly. "Karen and I decided there was no point in staying around there if Jeremy wasn't there, so we started to leave the hospital."

"But then this lady called us," Karen injected.

66

"This Mrs. Swartz?" Dave wanted to know.

"Yes, Mrs. Swartz called and wanted to talk to us." Mr. Tyler's face was radiant as he reviewed the events.

"How come she called you?" Roy wanted to know. "She didn't know you, did she?"

"No," he said slowly. "But that's the wonderful part about the way our Lord leads. This lady wanted to express her concern to us over Jeremy."

"How'd she know about him?" Dave continued to question.

"She had overheard us talking to the receptionist and wanted us to know that she understood what we were going through," his father replied.

"But how come?" Dave asked again, a bewildered look on his face.

"Her son is in the hospital because of meningitis, and—" Mr. Tyler began.

"Two of them in one day?" Roy interrupted. "That's almost an epidemic, isn't it?"

"No," Karen said, shaking her head. "Maybe Jeremy doesn't have meningitis. Maybe he just—" She stopped abruptly.

"Oh, boy," Dave injected. "Have you ever lost me!"

Mr. Tyler saw the frustration on both Karen's and Dave's faces.

"Let me try to explain," he said. Then, starting from the beginning, he told Roy and Dave all that had happened—how the little boy the police were looking for was actually Billy Swartz and how it was possible that Jeremy might not be seriously ill at all.

"You see," he finished. "The police officer told us about only one case—Billy Swartz."

Dave Tyler turned and looked at his sister.

"But Karen," he said, "What about the baby's crying and being sick and stuff? And what about the camper taking off in the middle of the night?"

Karen turned and faced her dad. For the moment she had forgotten that the problem of the old tag-along camper and the baby had not been solved at all. Even though Billy Swartz was being cared for in the hospital, Jeremy still had not been found. Maybe he too was suffering from this serious illness.

"Of course," Mr. Tyler began, "we don't know that she got up and left in the middle of the night. She could have pulled out ten minutes before we got up, you know."

But Dave didn't buy that idea. And neither did Karen.

Mr. Tyler spoke again.

"You know, we may never see Jeremy and his mother again," he said seriously. "But wherever they are, they are actually responsible for the fact that we were able to lead a young mother to the Lord Jesus. Do you realize that?"

Karen thought about that for a long time. What her father had said was true. It was because of little, sick Jeremy that Mrs. Swartz found the Lord. But what about Jeremy? Didn't God care just as much for him? And if He did, why wouldn't He let them find the sick baby and his mother? Suddenly she could hear her father's voice as he quoted one of his favorite mottoes: "God works in mysterious ways His wonders to perform."

"Please, God," Karen prayed silently. "Please work for Jeremy too."

Chapter 10

"There's a Camper Up Ahead"

Traffic on the highway was a little heavier than it had been earlier when the group first left the camping area. Mr. Tyler's attention was given to the driving, but Roy and Dave continued a constant chatter about everything that had happened so far on the trip. They discussed the excitement of helping at the Bible camp and some of the scenic things they would be enjoying during their free hours. But Karen was quiet. She was just as happy as the others at the conversion of Mrs. Swartz, maybe more happy since she had been there. And she, too, was looking forward to camp and hoping to see some exciting places of interest. But there was still Jeremy.

She wished now that she had just come out and asked the lady what was wrong with her little boy. She had been stupid to invite her to supper and then leave like she did. But then, she had promised Dave and her dad that she wouldn't get nosey.

"I sure hope he's all right," she said aloud, forgetting for the moment that nobody else in the car had been talking about little Jeremy.

Mr. Tyler turned and faced her for a quick second.

"Oh, I'm sure he will be," he said confidently. "Mrs. Swartz said the doctor had given her every hope that Billy will recover."

Karen shook her head determinedly.

"Oh, no," she said, speaking louder than she had intended. "I wasn't thinking about Billy."

"Oh," Mr. Tyler replied. He said no more until after he had looked into the rearview mirror and signaled to pass the slow truck in front of them. "You were talking about Jeremy?"

Karen nodded silently.

By this time Roy and Dave were giving their attention to Karen too.

"Sure makes you wonder what happened to them and where they are," Roy said, a dull sound to his voice, "doesn't it?"

"I still can't figure out why that lady would tag us the way she did yesterday and then leave before we did today," Dave added. "It doesn't add up."

Karen turned quickly and looked out the side window. A tear trickled down her cheek. She was still deeply concerned for the little baby she had seen. And that didn't make sense. She didn't even know the people. Why would she have such a keen feeling for them? Somehow she couldn't share her real concern with anyone—except the Lord. She prayed silently for a long time, asking God to be with Jeremy and his mother, wherever they were.

Roy's voice brought her back to reality.

"Hey!" he called loudly. "There's a camper up ahead. It looks like it's in the ditch."

Karen stared ahead through the windshield. Her father began to slow down even though he was some distance from the parked vehicle.

"I don't think it's in the ditch," he said, trying to hold his own car on the road and still keep an eye on the camper.

"We'd better stop, Dad," Karen ordered, not realizing how demanding her voice sounded. "It could be Jeremy and his mother. And maybe they need help."

Dave, who had become interested too, agreed.

"Yeah," he said. "She could have a flat tire or something."

Karen turned briefly to face her brother, admiration in her face. Up until this morning Dave had not seemed concerned about either the camper or its occupants; he had, in fact, teased her so much that he seemed almost indifferent about the whole matter. But ever since the hospital stop, he had been different.

Mr. Tyler looked for a spot to park, but there was no room behind the old camper.

"Boy, she just barely missed the edge of that ditch," he said. He drove on ahead to find a place where he could pull off.

"It does look something like that lady's camper," Roy said, the slightest hint of doubt in his statement.

"Oh, it's hers all right," Karen insisted. "I ought to know; I got a close look at it when I went to invite her to supper."

Dave laughed lightly. "You're right. You should know it. You've been staring at it ever since we left Trendale."

Karen squirmed nervously as her dad tried to find a place to safely park the station wagon. She looked back again. There was no question in her mind—that was the same camper that had been following them all day yesterday.

Karen hardly waited for her father to set the brake on the car before she opened the door and started to run toward the old vehicle.

71

"I hope they're OK," Roy said breathlessly, trying to keep up with Karen.

Before she could answer, he called out. "This is the license number all right. I memorized it while I was watching it follow us."

Karen had not given that much thought to the license plate, though she did remember that it was from another state. She knocked loudly on the door.

"Hello in there," she called, taking a step back. "Do you need help?"

By this time Mr. Tyler and Dave had arrived.

"Everything all right?" Mr. Tyler asked, scanning the camper with a quick, sweeping glance.

Karen knocked again, much louder this time.

"Jeremy's mother," she called, not knowing what other name to use.

"There's no answer," Roy said, feeling that someone should reply to Mr. Tyler's question.

"Have you tried the door?" Dave asked.

Karen shook her head and placed her hand on the door handle. She gave it a slight pull, then another much firmer one.

"It's locked," she said, a disappointed tone in her voice.

Mr. Tyler shook his head.

"Well, that makes sense," he said slowly. "Certainly no one would walk off and leave their camper unlocked."

"Not even an antique like this," Dave finished for him, laughing as he spoke.

Karen looked pleadingly into her father's face.

"Dad," she nearly cried. "Where is she?"

He shook his head slowly, a look of frustration in his eyes.

72

"I'm sorry, Honey," he confessed. "I wouldn't have any idea." He turned and began to walk around the camper, stopping to check each tire carefully. Karen followed him part of the way and then went back to try again at the locked door.

"Should I knock again?" she asked, knowing full well there was no one in the camper.

Roy shook his head. "They would have answered by now," he said. "Unless they're too sick or hurt."

She sucked in her breath and turned again to her father. That thought had not occurred to Karen.

"Oh, Dad," she said, a new concern in her voice. "How can we know for sure she's not in there?"

Dave had an idea. "I know," he said. Walking to the front of the vehicle, he jumped up on the bumper and looked in, cupping his hands above his eyes.

"Do you see anything?" Karen asked impatiently.

"Looks pretty dark," he called back. "But I don't think anyone's in there."

By this time both Mr. Tyler and Roy had climbed up and were looking in too.

"It's pretty hard to see anything," Mr. Tyler said.

Roy agreed. "But I think it's empty."

Karen breathed a sigh of relief. If they weren't in there, they probably weren't sick or hurt. But still the concern continued to build in her mind. Just because they weren't there didn't mean they were all right. The very fact that they were gone was one indication that something had happened. Maybe Jeremy got worse—whatever was wrong ith him. Oh, why hadn't she asked the lady about it when she had talked to her?

A car pulled up across the road, but Karen hardly noticed. Instead she continued to gaze at the others who were still trying to spot some indication of activity in the old camper.

Before she knew it, a tall police officer was standing beside her.

"You folks searching this vehicle for any special reason?" he asked. There was a decided note of suspicion in his voice.

At the sound of the strange voice, Mr. Tyler and the two boys jumped down and stood sheepishly staring into the face of the highway patrolman.

Chapter 11

"Jeremy—He's Sick"

Karen Tyler whirled, facing the police officer. Then just as quickly she turned to look at her father.

Mr. Tyler took a step forward and stood before the patrolman.

"We were trying to see if there was anyone in the camper," he explained lamely. "We were afraid they might be hurt." But even as he spoke, the others saw the look of suspicion on the officer's face.

"And there isn't anyone inside, is there?" he questioned knowingly.

"It's too dark in there to see very well," Roy broke in.

"And the door's locked," Dave added, turning to point toward the camper entrance.

Karen wished she could think of something vital to add, but she couldn't. Instead she stood there nervously, wondering if the police officer actually thought they had been trying to break into the deserted camper.

"We know the lady who owns this," she finally managed and then half-whispered, "sort of."

The patrolman caught it.

"Sort of?" he probed. Then before anyone could explain, he asked still another question. This time

re seemed to be a genuine friendliness to his
oice.

"You people friends of the lady?" he asked
evenly.

Mr. Tyler shook his head. "No," he admitted.
"We've just been traveling together."

The officer seemed confused.

"You don't know her, but you're traveling together?" he stated, a definite question in his voice.

"She's been following us," Karen pointed out.
Her voice rose in a high crescendo.

The police officer turned and looked around.

"That your car?" he asked, pointing to the station wagon parked down the road.

Mr. Tyler nodded.

"That's right. We stopped, thinking perhaps the
lady had a flat tire or something."

"Yeah," Roy broke in. "We just wanted to help."

Karen Tyler stood by silently as her father and
the policeman carried on a detailed conversation.
Mr. Tyler explained how they had noticed the
camper following them all day yesterday. He told
the uniformed man about stopping at the campsite
and how the lady was gone early this morning
when they awakened. He even explained how concerned Karen had been when she learned that the
little child was sick.

"That's the lady all right," the officer said after
Mr. Tyler had finished.

"You mean you know where she is?" Karen
injected, even before the officer had completed his
sentence.

He nodded. There was a much friendlier look on
his face now that he no longer seemed to question
their interest in the camper.

76

"I took her up the road to a garage in town," he said simply. "Fan belt broke." He pointed to the old camper. "And wouldn't you know it, they didn't have this size on hand. So she's sitting it out until they can find one."

Mr. Tyler seemed concerned.

"Is she still there?" he asked.

"Far as I know," the patrolman replied. "I asked her if there was some place I could take her, but all she wants is to get this thing fixed and get on the road again. Has some special reason for wanting to get home today."

"How's she going to get back out here to her camper?" Dave asked, showing as much concern as the others.

"Oh, I think Charlie will bring her out," the officer assured them. "He'll put the belt on and see that she gets on her way again."

Karen breathed deeply.

"Was her little baby OK?" she asked, still wondering about Jeremy's condition.

"Pretty fussy," the officer said. Then he shook his head. "That little lady shouldn't have been on the road alone. I'm not surprised she tagged behind you like she did."

Mr. Tyler shook his head and looked straight into the face of the patrolman.

"I'm surprised her husband would let her travel so far alone. I won't let my wife do that."

"She had no choice," the officer said sympathetically. "Lost her husband in a car accident less than a month ago. Decided to move back to Arizona now, I guess."

Karen's mouth dropped open in shock.

77

"What happened?" She was nearly in tears. "To her husband."

"She told me he was killed when a drunk came up over the hill on the wrong side of the road." The patrolman paused briefly and shook his head. "Those drunks never learn. He came out without a scratch, but he totaled their car and took her husband's life, just like that." He snapped his fingers as he spoke. "Guess it's just lucky he was traveling alone, or this little lady wouldn't be on the road today."

A sick feeling came over Karen as she listened to the policeman's report.

"That poor lady," Roy was saying.

"Well," the policeman said, taking another deep breath. "She said her neighbors tried to discourage her from making the trip in this old camper, but with the car demolished, this was all she had. And she wanted to get back to her relatives in Arizona—by today. She's been lucky so far; this fan belt's the first thing that's gone wrong."

As he spoke, a truck from the service station pulled up across the road directly behind the policeman's car.

"Well, here they come now," the patrolman said, watching as two men jumped out of the truck.

"Where's Jeremy and his mother?" Karen asked, looking first at her father and then back toward the truck.

"Yeah," Roy added. "How's she going to get back here so she can get her camper? I thought she'd be riding out with them."

"Hi there," one of the men said. Then without waiting for anyone to speak, he laughed, "We'll get this baby rolling in just a couple of minutes."

78

The other man pulled out a set of keys, walked around to the camper door and unlocked it.

Dave Tyler followed him.

"Where's the lady who owns this camper?" he asked seriously, looking from one man to the other. "How come she didn't come out here with you?"

The man stepped aside and opened the door. "Her kid got sick," he explained off-handedly. "There's a doctor's office just up the street from the station, so we sent her up there."

Karen looked over at the man and just as quickly back to her father.

"Daddy!" she cried. "Jeremy—he's sick. Maybe real sick, like Billy."

Mr. Tyler went over and put his arm around his daughter's shoulders.

"Now, Karen," he said calmly. "Let's not imagine the worst. Let's trust God for the best."

"But, Daddy," Karen cried. "He's . . ." Her voice trailed off into nothing.

Chapter 12

A Sincere Prayer

Karen Tyler pulled at her father's shirt sleeve.

"Dad," she said pleadingly. "Let's go and see if everything's OK with Jeremy and his mother." Distress flashed from her eyes. "Maybe he's got meningitis too," she finished.

"Meningitis?" the officer asked. "Another one? I was looking for a lady and her son this morning. But they checked into the hospital before we could find them."

"Mrs. Swartz?" Mr. Tyler asked.

"Yes," the patrolman answered. Then, shaking his head, he said, "Say, you seem to know everything and everyone in these parts. Not bad for a stranger." He laughed.

"We stopped and visited them," Mr. Tyler replied.

"Billy," Karen said softly.

"Right," the officer said. "But I haven't had a report on any other meningitis cases."

The man working on the camper's fan belt stopped and walked over to where the others were standing.

"You mean that little baby's got an infectious disease?" he asked, a sound of concern in his voice.

Mr. Tyler shook his head.

"We don't know that," he said slowly. "My daughter heard the radio announcement last night, and she thought maybe it was Jeremy."

Karen wondered if her father was as convinced that Jeremy was not seriously ill as he was trying to make it sound.

"I saw Jeremy last night," she added. "And he was runing a fever, so I sort of thought he could be awfully sick."

The serviceman shook his head in bewilderment and went back to work on the fan belt. Then he stood upright again.

"Could be," he said finally. "The little guy was sure fussy. And his mother did say he had a fever."

"Dad," Karen repeated for the second time. "Shouldn't we go and check it out and see for sure that he's all right?"

As she spoke, the service attendant put his tool-box away.

"Well, we're through here," he said.

The sound of the radio from the patrol car caught the attention of the officer.

"Excuse me," he said, turning to face Mr. Tyler. "I'd better get that call." He walked across the road, opened the door to his car and got in. In a few minutes he called to them.

"Another call," he said, waving. With that, he started his car and drove away.

Karen watched the car for a minute.

"Mike here can drive the camper," Charlie, the serviceman, called. "That way I'll be right behind him with the truck in case anything falls apart." He laughed loudly. But all Karen could think about was the poor lady whose husband had been killed and who now had only her baby and an old run-down camper. It didn't seem at all humorous to her.

"All set," Mike called as he pulled the camper

out onto the highway. Charlie got into the truck, made a quick U-turn and followed close behind. Quickly, Mr. Tyler and his passengers got into the station wagon and followed the men into town.

"Boy," Roy sighed once they were on their way, "if our trip so far is any indication of the excitement we're going to have at Bible camp, I'm not sure I'm going to be able to handle it."

Dave smiled broadly.

"I don't know how anything more exciting could happen."

Karen turned quickly and looked at her father.

"We didn't get the address of the doctor," she said with concern. "How are we going to find them?"

Dave tapped his sister on the back.

"We're following the guys who are going to take us there, remember?" There was a slight bit of irritation in his voice.

"They're just going to the service station," Karen corrected.

Mr. Tyler interrupted her sentence.

"But they told us the doctor's office was just up the street from their station," he explained calmly. "They'll tell us how to get there."

That seemed to satisfy Karen for the moment.

"She'll have to get back to the service station to pick up the camper, won't she?" she asked suddenly.

Mr. Tyler nodded.

"Don't worry, Honey," he said kindly, anticipating her next question. "We won't leave until we've seen that they're OK."

Karen sat back, content for the moment. As she

did, Dave leaned up against the back of the seat in front of him.

"You know something, Karen?" he said, giving his sister another poke in the back.

She turned to face him, somehow sensing that he was going to scold her.

"You've got to quit making big deals about everything," he said, looking straight into her face. He laughed loudly. "You thought this woman might be a kidnapper and a hostage and all kinds of stuff, and here she is, a poor widow with a sick baby."

Karen swallowed hard. What Dave said was true. She did tend to look at the dark side of things. Her dad and mother had talked with her about it many times. And she had prayed about it too. But here she was, doing it again during this trip. But the fact remained that Jeremy was sick, and they didn't know what was wrong with him.

Roy broke into her silent thoughts.

"Well, Karen," he began slowly. "At least you were right when you insisted that we go to that hospital."

She turned and shot a grateful smile at Roy.

"If we hadn't gone there," Roy continued, not daring to look at Dave, "that Mrs. Swartz probably wouldn't be a Christian now."

Mr. Tyler kept his eyes on the truck ahead of them, but he whispered softly, " 'All things work together for good to them that love God, to them who are the called according to his purpose.' "

Dave shrugged indifferently.

"All of this is true," he reluctantly confessed. "I know that. But someday Karen's going to become very rich."

Karen turned suddenly to look at her brother.

"What in the world made you say a dumb thing like that?" she asked. "And what's money got to do with what we're talking about?"

"Someday," Dave smirked, "my sister is going to be a rich mystery writer, that's what."

Everyone in the station wagon laughed pleasantly.

Even though Mr. Tyler followed some distance behind the truck and the camper, he made sure he did not lose sight of them. While the two boys in the backseat of the station wagon continued their conversation, Karen began to think of all the things she could write about if she were a writer. The boys had been right. They had expected a lot of excitement after they arrived at the Bible camp, but it was strange that all these things were happening even before they got there.

Karen thought about them, one by one. Each thing had seemed to affect her more than the other. She became very serious. Was God trying to reach her through these incidents? Was He trying to tell her something? Her dad had said many times that the Lord often uses situations and circumstances to get the attention of His children. Maybe that's what God was doing now. Maybe He was trying to get her attention. Silently she thought about each happening and wondered what lessons she should be learning. God had allowed this lady to follow them for a reason, that was for sure. That's where it had all begun.

Karen closed her eyes and offered a sincere prayer to the Lord. "If You're trying to get through to me," she prayed silently, "please help me to listen."

As she thought about it, she realized that her Christian life had certainly not been anything to brag about lately. She recalled how her parents had wanted her to sign up to teach in this Bible camp long before she had agreed. But she had steadily refused. And even when she did finally agree, it was just because Mrs. Black had called and made her feel so needed. Karen was not very proud of herself for the way she had been living her Christian life lately. For some reason, she always seemed to put her own desires first. God came in second. When she thought about all her Lord had done for her, it made her even more ashamed.

Karen rehearsed the many things in her life that surely could not be pleasing to God. One thing was the way she treated her folks. She often talked back to them and let them know that she considered them old-fashioned and not with it—and all because they had one idea and she had another. A couple of verses flashed into her mind: "Children, obey your parents in the Lord: for this is right. Honour thy father and mother."

And her actions toward Dave weren't any better. He teased her a lot, and she seemed to take everything so seriously. That was the thing that usually brought about her harsh words. And these things were sin, she knew that.

"O, dear Lord," she continued sincerely and silently, "I'm so ashamed and so sorry." She paused. "Make this a very important week in my Christian life," she finished.

As she looked up, she noted that the truck and the camper were both signaling a left turn into the town. Her father followed them on to the service station. Even as she watched, a feeling of peace came over her, something that had been missing for a long time.

"Maybe when I see Jeremy's mother, I can talk to her about the Lord," she said aloud as they were nearing the station.

Mr. Tyler flashed a smile toward his daughter.

"Maybe that's what this is all about," he replied. "God always works things out for good, you know."

She nodded. "I know."

Mr. Tyler pulled up to the service garage and parked directly behind the other two vehicles. He got out of the station wagon and went in to talk to Charlie. Karen, Dave and Roy stepped out of the car and followed him.

"I'd like to pay the bill for this work," Mr. Tyler said to the man.

The attendant seemed a little shocked but said nothing. He wrote out a ticket and gave it to Karen's father.

"And I suppose you want to know where the doctor's office is too," the other attendant smiled.

"Right," replied Mr. Tyler.

The small group listened carefully as the man pointed to a building just two blocks away.

Everyone started out the door, and then Mr. Tyler stopped. He turned to Charlie.

"Any chance of us driving the camper to the doctor's office so it'll be there when the lady gets out?" he asked.

The other man pulled a set of keys out of his pocket and gave them to Charlie.

"I wouldn't ordinarily do this," Charlie said, tossing the keys to Karen's father. "But anyone

86

who'd drive a car with a church name on it and then pay a stranger's bill like you've done, well, I guess we can trust you."

They laughed heartily.

Mike put his hand on Mr. Tyler's arm. "Anyway," he said, pointing, "we can see old Doc's office from here. We'll know if you do what you say you're going to do."

They laughed again and walked back out to the two parked vehicles.

"Want me to drive the camper?" Roy asked, holding out his hands for the keys. Mr. Tyler threw them to the older boy and then got into the station wagon and led the way to the doctor's office. Karen turned and watched as the familiar camper left the station and followed behind them.

"Well," said Mr. Tyler, looking through the rearview mirror, "it feels good to see the camper behind us again, doesn't it?"

Karen nodded. She felt good too, not only because the old camper was following them again but also because she had made things right with the Lord. Her life was going to be different now and so was her ministry at the Bible camp.

In spite of the warmth from the summer sun that was flowing into the car, Karen shivered involuntarily. She still could not help but be concerned about Jeremy. The poor little guy had lost his father and was traveling with a brokenhearted mother. And on top of all that, he was sick, maybe seriously sick.

Chapter 13

It Couldn't Be!

Dave Tyler and Roy Sparton had just parked the camper and walked over to the station wagon when the door of the doctor's office opened. The mysterious lady stepped out, holding her young son.

Karen opened the door on her side of the car, got out quickly and ran toward the lady.

"Hi," she said in an excited and friendly tone.

The woman seemed genuinely pleased and surprised to see her. She shifted her child into her other arm and held out a hand to Karen.

"I didn't think I'd ever see you again," she said pleasantly, "especially after all the things that have happened to me today."

Suddenly she spotted the camper.

"Oh, how nice," she called out. "They delivered it."

By this time Mr. Tyler, Dave and Roy had reached her too.

"We got to deliver it," Roy said, giving her the keys to the camper.

"And there's no charge," Dave added.

The woman seemed frustrated. She looked from one member of the small group to another.

"But there must be a charge," she challenged. "That man had to drive all the way out of town to get my camper, and—" She stopped and looked at Mr. Tyler.

He flashed a pleasant smile back at her.

"It's all taken care of," he admitted. "So you're all set to be on your way again."

"But, Dad," Karen said, raising her voice above the street noise. For a moment she was afraid her dad was encouraging the lady to leave before they could find out if her little boy was all right. "We have to find out about Jeremy."

"Jeremy?" the lady asked. "What about him?" A look of distress came across her face.

"Is he all right?" Karen asked, looked directly at the little baby.

"Well, yes, under the circumstances," the lady answered.

There! It was true. Jeremy was sick and no doubt in worse condition than the woman seemed to realize.

"Do you have to take him to the hospital?" Roy broke in, sharing Karen's concern.

The woman looked utterly confused.

"Hospital?" she repeated. "Why, no, the doctor didn't think it was too serious."

"But he should get treatment as soon as he can," Karen insisted. "Meningitis is—" She didn't get to finish because the young mother interrupted.

"Meningitis!" the woman called out. "Jeremy doesn't have meningitis!"

"But he's sick," Karen persisted. "You said so last night."

"And you told the mechanic that he had a fever and that you had to get him to the doctor," Roy stated.

The woman smiled broadly.

"You know a lot about me, don't you?" she said pleasantly. She paused for a brief moment. "Jeremy is getting another tooth," she said proudly. "And this morning he was very fussy, even running a fever. I've been giving him aspirin, but that didn't seem to be doing enough, so I wanted a doctor to look at him."

"And he's all right?" Mr. Tyler asked, a fatherly sound to his voice.

"As all right as any one-year-old child who's cutting a new tooth can be," she replied. A serious look came over her face. "A year old today," she mused.

"Jeremy's birthday is today?" Karen asked excitedly. "Shouldn't we celebrate or something?"

Mr. Tyler smiled broadly. "That's a wonderful idea; we always did that for our children. Why don't we find some nice place for dinner?"

Suddenly the young mother brightened.

"You know something? We've been talking all this time, and I'm about to have dinner with you, and I don't even know who you nice people are."

Mr. Tyler laughed good-naturedly.

"Well, we can remedy that," he said, holding out his hand to the woman. "I'm Robert Tyler, and these two, Dave and Karen, are my children." He pointed to Dave and Karen and then turned to Roy. "This is Dave's friend, Roy Sparton. We're on our way to the Phoenix area."

"And I'm Maria Carlson," the woman volunteered. "I'm on my way to my parents' home. I may move back there."

Karen nodded. "Yes, that's what we heard."

There was more excitement and talking before Mr. Tyler finally suggested that they would be more comfortable talking around the dinner table.

"The boys can go with me," he suggested. "And, Karen, you ride with Mrs. Carlson. That way you can take care of the baby while she's driving."

Karen agreed wholeheartedly, and Mrs. Carlson smiled too.

"Oh, that would be nice," she said. "Jeremy hates being strapped down while I'm driving."

There was a quick hustle to the vehicles. Karen Tyler seated herself in the old camper with Jeremy Carlson on her lap.

"He's sure a cute baby," Karen said, holding his small hands in hers.

Mrs. Carlson smiled. "A perfect image of his father," she said. And then, as though no one was listening, she added softly, "I wish his daddy could see him today—Jeremy's first birthday."

Karen felt herself emotionally choked up when she remembered what had happened to the young child's father.

"That policeman who drove you to town," Karen began. "He told us all about your husband's accident."

Jeremy became a little restless, and Mrs. Carlson glanced quickly at him but said nothing. It was obvious that she was missing her husband.

"A drunk driver," Karen finished as she talked about Mr. Carlson's accident and death.

The woman nodded. "Yes," she said sadly, "and still they let young people drink." A tear trickled down her face.

Karen hardly knew what to say.

"I'm sorry," she apologized. "I shouldn't have said anything about it."

"Oh, no," the lady brightened. "I like to talk

about Eric. I loved him very much, and I find a great deal of comfort in talking about him."

Karen Tyler straightened. Suddenly she remembered how she had asked God for a chance to talk to this lady about the Lord. And now, here it was—a wide open opportunity. Mrs. Carlson had made it for her. Karen opened her mouth to say something, but the words refused to come out. She would try again. She had to tell the woman about the real Comforter, the Lord Jesus. She hesitated again, and before she could start, the woman began the conversation herself.

"Talking about Eric," she began softly, "and talking with my Lord have been two things that have helped me more than anything. That and reading my Bible," she finished.

Karen's mouth dropped open.

"You're—you're a Christian?" she asked bluntly.

Mrs. Carlson smiled. "Oh, yes," she assured the Tyler girl. "And if I hadn't known the Lord during these days, I'm not sure how I could have made it."

Karen laughed aloud. As she did, Jeremy looked up into her face and smiled broadly.

"Something strike you funny?" Mrs. Carlson asked, smiling in spite of her tears.

"Yes, me!" Karen confessed. "I promised God that if we could find you, I would make it a point to talk with you about the Lord, to tell you about being a Christian. But you're the one talking about Him before I could even get up enough courage to say anything."

By this time they had reached the restaurant.

"Daddy," Karen called as soon as the others were out of the station wagon. "Mrs. Carlson is a Christian too."

Mr. Tyler smiled. "You know, I thought you were," he said with assurance. "I had determined to talk with you about it over dinner," he admitted. "That was one reason I was hoping you would accept our invitation to be our guest."

Maria Carlson took her young son in her arms and followed the others to a quiet table.

"God certainly works in mysterious ways," she began when they were seated. She paused briefly. "You know, my parents were a little concerned about my traveling alone on such a long trip," she stated. "But I told them I had prayed and asked God to send someone to help me. And He did—you folks."

The group talked on for several more minutes, but finally Roy Sparton could contain himself no longer. There was still one question that had not been answered.

"But how come you got up and left before we did this morning?" he asked bluntly. "You'd been following us up to that point."

Mrs. Carlson smiled.

"Well, for one thing, I felt I was close enough to home now to be pretty safe." She stopped and took a deep breath. "But that wasn't the main reason. Jeremy had been fussing most of the night, and I thought if I could get home before the heat of the day, he would feel better."

"And then you had car trouble," Dave inserted.

Maria Carlson nodded, taking another deep breath.

"Yes," she confessed. "And did I ever wish I'd stayed behind you then."

The waitress brought Jeremy a high chair and

93

then took their orders. When she left, Mrs. Carlson began to talk again.

"After my husband died," she said softly, "I remembered how we had planned to go and visit Jeremy's grandparents on his first birthday." She stopped and took a drink from the glass in front of her. "Without Eric, I wasn't sure I could handle that long trip by myself. So I asked the Lord to let me find someone I could follow—and trust."

Karen flashed a look at Dave, but she said nothing.

"I stopped in a small town called Trendale to get gas," Mrs. Carlson continued.

"That's our town," Karen broke in. "That's where we live."

If the woman was surprised, she did not show it.

"As I left the city limits, I spotted your station wagon with the church name on it."

"And you felt we were the answer to your prayers?" Roy asked, still stunned by the woman's touching testimony.

She nodded, a smile playing on her face.

"I was confident that God had brought us together. So I just made it a point to stay close behind you—a real tagalong."

"Gas stops and all," Dave added, making his words sound like an apology to his sister.

"Yes," laughed the woman. "That station you stopped at yesterday sold the only kind of gas Eric ever used in our family car." She paused again. "I sat in the camper and just thanked the Lord for taking care of me the way He did."

Dave Tyler began to laugh. "Do you know what my sister had you figured to be?"

94

Karen stopped him abruptly. Then she turned to face Mrs. Carlson.

"I thought there was someone else traveling with you," she said lamely.

Mr. Tyler felt it was time to change the subject.

"How much farther do you have to go?" Mr. Tyler asked, looking at his watch and checking their own schedule in his mind.

"It's a long drive," she said. "My parents live at a Bible camp just outside Phoenix and—"

"Bible camp? Outside of Phoenix?" Karen broke in. It couldn't be! Were they all headed for the same camp?

Before the young mother could answer, Mr. Tyler spoke up. "You aren't Chester Black's daughter, are you?" he asked incredulously.

Mrs. Carlson nodded. "Yes, I'm Maria Black Carlson," she replied. "And Jeremy and I are going back home."

Tears came to the eyes of everyone seated around the table—even Dave. God had certainly brought them together in an unusual way.

When dinner was finished, Karen got into the old camper with Jeremy and his mother, and the others got into the station wagon. There were many miles left before they would all arrive at camp. No doubt there would be some wonderful experiences there, too, but probably none more exciting than those that had already taken place. Karen thought about Mrs. Swartz, a new believer, and about how her own life had been challenged and changed.

As both vehicles started again, one thing was very different. Maria Carlson pulled out first, leading the way. This time it wasn't the mysterious camper but the well-marked church station wagon that tagged along.